"RING FOR YOUR MAID, AND WHEN SHE COMES IN WE'LL POUNCE UPON HER AND TEAR OFF HER FACE. I'LL WEAR HER FACE TONIGHT INSTEAD OF MINE."

LEONORA CARRINGTON
Born 1917, Lancashire, United Kingdom
Died 2011, Mexico City, Mexico

'The Skeleton's Holiday' was written in 1939 as part of a
collaborative novel with Hans Arp, Marcel Duchamp, Paul
Eluard, Max Ernst, Georges Hugnet, Gisèle Prassinos et al.,
called *The Man Who Lost His Skeleton*. 'Uncle Sam Carrington',
'The Debutante', 'White Rabbits', 'Seventh Horse', 'My Flannel
Knickers' and 'The Oval Lady' were translated into English
from the original French by Kathrine Talbot, Marina Warner,
Paul de Angelis and Carrington herself and first published
in 1988.

•

CARRINGTON IN PENGUIN MODERN CLASSICS
The Hearing Trumpet

LEONORA CARRINGTON

The Skeleton's Holiday

PENGUIN BOOKS

PENGUIN CLASSICS

UK | USA | Canada | Ireland | Australia
India | New Zealand | South Africa

Penguin Books is part of the Penguin Random House group
of companies whose addresses can be found at
global.penguinrandomhouse.com.

First published 1989
This selection first published 2018
001

Set in 12/15 pt Dante MT Std
Typeset by Jouve (UK), Milton Keynes
Printed in Great Britain by Clays Ltd, St Ives plc

ISBN: 978–0241–33916–9

Contents

White Rabbits

The time has come that I must tell the events which began in 40 Pest Street. The houses, which were reddish-black, looked as if they had issued mysteriously from the fire of London. The house in front of my window, covered with an occasional wisp of creeper, was as black and empty-looking as any plague-ridden residence subsequently licked by flames and smoke. This is not the way that I had imagined New York.

It was so hot that I got palpitations when I ventured out into the streets, so I sat and considered the house opposite and occasionally bathed my sweating face.

The light was never very strong in Pest Street. There was always a reminiscence of smoke, which made visibility troubled and hazy – still it was possible to study the house opposite carefully, even precisely. Besides, my eyes have always been excellent.

I spent several days watching for some sort of movement opposite but there was none, and I finally took to undressing quite freely before my open window and doing breathing exercises optimistically in the thick Pest Street air. This must have made my lungs as black as the houses.

One afternoon I washed my hair and sat out on the diminutive stone crescent which served as a balcony to dry it. I hung my head between my knees and watched a bluebottle suck the dry corpse of a spider between my feet. I looked up through my long hair and saw something black in the sky, ominously quiet for an airplane. Parting my hair, I was in time to see a large raven alight on the balcony of the house opposite. It sat on the balustrade and seemed to peer into the empty window. Then it poked its head under its wing, apparently searching for lice. A few minutes later I was not unduly surprised to see the double windows open and admit a woman onto the balcony. She carried a large dish full of bones, which she emptied onto the floor. With a short appreciative squeak, the raven hopped down and poked about amongst its unpleasant repast.

The woman, who had very long black hair, used

her hair to wipe out the dish. Then she looked straight at me and smiled in a friendly fashion. I smiled back and waved a towel. This served to encourage her, for she tossed her head coquettishly and gave me a very elegant salute after the fashion of a queen.

'Do you happen to have any bad meat over there that you don't need?' she called.

'Any what?' I called back, wondering if my ears had deceived me.

'Any stinking meat? Decomposed flesh meat?'

'Not at the moment,' I replied, wondering if she was trying to be funny.

'Won't you have any towards the end of the week? If so, I would be very grateful if you would bring it over.'

Then she stepped back into the empty window and disappeared. The raven flew away.

My curiosity about the house and its occupant prompted me to buy a large lump of meat the following day. I set it on the balcony on a bit of newspaper and awaited developments. In a comparatively short time the smell was so strong that I was obliged to pursue my daily activities with a strong paperclip on the end of my nose. Occasionally I descended into the street to breathe.

Towards Thursday evening I noticed that the meat was changing colour, so waving aside a flight of rancorous bluebottles, I scooped it into my sponge bag and set out for the house opposite. I noticed, descending the stairs, that the landlady seemed to avoid me.

It took me some time to find the front door of the house opposite. It turned out to be hidden under a cascade of something, giving the impression that nobody had been either in or out of this house for years. The bell was of the old-fashioned kind that you pull, and when I pulled it rather harder than I intended, it came right off in my hand. I gave the door an angry push and it caved inwards, admitting a ghastly smell of putrid meat. The hall, which was almost dark, seemed to be of carved woodwork.

The woman herself came rustling down the stairs, carrying a torch.

'How do you do? How do you do?' she murmured ceremoniously, and I was surprised to notice that she wore an ancient beautiful dress of green silk. But as she approached me I saw that her skin was dead white and glittered as if speckled with thousands of minute stars.

It's twenty-odd years since I've seen a new face. Besides, she's brought meat for the rabbits.'

She turned and beckoned me to her side. 'You want to stay with us, do you not, my dear?' I was suddenly clutched by fear and I wanted to get out and away from those terrible silver people and the white carnivorous rabbits.

'I think I must be going, it's supper time –'

The man on the chair gave a shrill peal of laughter, terrifying the rabbit on his knee, which sprang to the floor and disappeared.

The woman thrust her face so near to mine that her sickly breath seemed to anaesthetize me. 'Do you not want to stay and become like us? In seven years your skin will be like stars, in seven little years you will have the holy disease of the Bible, leprosy!'

I stumbled and ran, choking with horror; some unholy curiosity made me look over my shoulder as I reached the front door and I saw her waving her hand over the banister, and as she waved it, her fingers fell off and dropped to the ground like shooting stars.

Uncle Sam Carrington

Whenever Uncle Sam Carrington saw the full moon he couldn't stop laughing. A sunset had the same effect on Aunt Edgeworth. Between them they caused my poor mother a great deal of suffering, for she had a certain social reputation to keep up. When I was eight I was considered the most serious member of my family. My mother confided in me. She told me that it was a crying shame that she wasn't invited anywhere, that Lady Cholmondeley-Bottom cut her when they passed in the street. I was grief-stricken.

Uncle Sam Carrington and Aunt Edgeworth lived at home. They lived on the first floor. So it was impossible to hide our sad state of affairs. For days I wondered how I could deliver my family from this disgrace. In the end I couldn't stand the tension and my mother's tears, they upset me too much. I decided to find a solution by myself.

One evening, when the sun had turned a brilliant red, and Aunt Edgeworth was giggling in a particularly outrageous manner, I took a pot of jam and a fishing hook and set off. I sang, 'Come into the garden, Maud, / For the black bat, night, has flown,' to frighten the bats away. My father used to sing that when he didn't go to church, or else he sang a song called 'It Cost Me Seven and Sixpence'. He sang both with equal feeling.

All right, I thought to myself, the journey has begun. The night will surely bring a solution. If I keep count of the trees until I reach the place I'm going to, I shan't get lost. I'll remember the number of trees on the return journey.

But I'd forgotten that I could only count to ten, and even then I made mistakes. In a very short time I'd counted to ten several times, and I'd gone completely astray. Trees surrounded me on all sides. 'I'm in a forest,' I said, and I was right.

The full moon shone brightly between the trees, so I was able to see, a few yards in front of me, the origins of a distressing noise. It was two cabbages having a terrible fight. They were tearing each other's leaves off with such ferocity that soon there was nothing but torn leaves everywhere and no cabbages.

'Never mind,' I told myself, 'it's only a nightmare.' But then I remembered that I'd never gone to bed that night, and so it couldn't possibly be a nightmare. 'That's awful.'

Thereupon I left the corpses and went on my way. Walking along I met a friend. It was the horse who, years later, was to play an important part in my life.

'Hello,' he said. 'Are you looking for something?' I explained to him the purpose of my late-night expedition.

'I can see that this is a very complicated matter from a social point of view,' he said. 'There are two ladies living near here who deal with such matters. Their aim is the extermination of family shame. They're expert at it. I'll take you to them if you like.'

The Misses Cunningham-Jones lived in a house discreetly surrounded by wild plants and under-clothes of bygone times. They were in the garden, playing a game of draughts. The horse stuck his head between the legs of a pair of 1890 bloomers and addressed the Misses Cunningham-Jones.

'Show your friend in,' said the lady sitting on the

right, speaking with a very distinguished accent. 'In the interest of respectability, we are always ready to come to the rescue.' The other lady inclined her head graciously. She was wearing an immense hat decorated with a great collection of horticultural specimens.

'Young lady,' she said, offering me a Louis Quinze chair, 'does your family descend from our dear departed Duke of Wellington? Or from Sir Walter Scott, that noble aristocrat of pure literature?'

I felt a bit embarrassed. There were no aristocrats in my family. She saw my hesitation and said with the most charming smile, 'My dear child, you must realize that here we deal only with the affairs of the oldest and most noble families of England.'

I had an inspiration, and my face lit up. 'In our dining-room at home . . .'

The horse kicked me hard in the backside. 'Never mention anything as vulgar as food,' he whispered.

Fortunately the ladies were slightly deaf. I immediately corrected myself. 'In our drawing-room,' I continued, confused, 'there is a table on which, we are told, a duchess forgot her lorgnette in 1700.'

'In that case,' one of the ladies said, 'we can perhaps settle the matter. Of course, we shall have to set a rather higher fee.

'Wait here for a few minutes, then we'll give you what you need. While you are waiting, you may look at the pictures in this book. It is instructive and interesting. No library is complete without it: my sister and I have always lived by its admirable example.'

The book was called *The Secrets of the Flowers of Refinement, or The Vulgarity of Food*.

When the two ladies had gone, the horse said, 'Do you know how to walk without making a sound?'

'Certainly,' I replied.

'Let's go and see the ladies at work,' he said. 'Come. But if you value your life, don't make the slightest noise.'

The ladies were in their kitchen garden. It was behind their house and was surrounded by a high brick wall. I climbed on the horse's back, and a pretty astonishing sight met my eyes: the Misses Cunningham-Jones, each armed with a huge whip, were whipping the vegetables on all sides, shouting, 'One's got to suffer to go to Heaven. Those who do not wear corsets will never get there.'

The vegetables, for their part, were fighting among

themselves, and the larger ones threw the smaller ones at the ladies with cries of hate.

'It's always like this,' said the horse in a low voice. 'The vegetables have to suffer for the sake of society. You'll see that they'll soon catch one for you, and that it'll die for the cause.'

The vegetables didn't look keen to die an honourable death, but the ladies were stronger. Soon two carrots and a courgette fell into their hands.

'Quick,' said the horse, 'let's go back.'

We had hardly got back and were sitting once more in front of *The Vulgarity of Food* when the two ladies returned, looking just about as poised as before. They gave me a parcel which contained the vegetables, and in return I paid them with the pot of jam and the fishing hook.

The Debutante

When I was a debutante, I often went to the zoo. I went so often that I knew the animals better than I knew girls of my own age. Indeed, it was in order to get away from people that I found myself at the zoo every day. The animal I got to know best was a young hyena. She knew me too. She was very intelligent. I taught her French, and she, in return, taught me her language. In this way we passed many pleasant hours.

My mother was arranging a ball in my honour on the first of May. During this time I was in a state of great distress for whole nights. I've always detested balls, especially when they are given in my honour. On the morning of the first of May 1934, very early, I went to visit the hyena.

'What a bloody nuisance,' I said to her. 'I've got to go to my ball tonight.'

'You're very lucky,' she said. 'I'd love to go. I don't

know how to dance, but at least I could make small talk.'

'There'll be a great many different things to eat,' I told her. 'I've seen truckloads of food delivered to our house.'

'And you're complaining,' replied the hyena, disgusted. 'Just think of me, I eat once a day, and you can't imagine what a heap of bloody rubbish I'm given.'

I had an audacious idea, and I almost laughed. 'All you have to do is to go instead of me!'

'We don't resemble each other enough, otherwise I'd gladly go,' said the hyena rather sadly.

'Listen,' I said. 'No one sees too well in the evening light. If you disguise yourself, nobody will notice you in the crowd. Besides, we're practically the same size. You're my only friend, I beg you to do this for me.'

She thought this over, and I knew that she really wanted to accept. 'Done,' she said all of a sudden.

There weren't many keepers about, it was so early in the morning. I opened the cage quickly, and in a very few moments we were out in the street. I hailed a taxi; at home, everybody was still in bed. In my room I brought out the dress I was to wear that evening. It was a little long, and the hyena found it

difficult to walk in my high-heeled shoes. I found
some gloves to hide her hands, which were too hairy
to look like mine. By the time the sun was shining
into my room, she was able to make her way around
the room several times, walking more or less upright.
We were so busy that my mother almost opened the
door to say good morning before the hyena had hidden under my bed.

'There's a bad smell in your room,' my mother
said, opening the window. 'You must have a scented
bath before tonight, with my new bath salts.'

'Certainly,' I said.

She didn't stay long. I think the smell was too
much for her. 'Don't be late for breakfast,' she said
and left the room.

The greatest difficulty was to find a way of dis-
guising the hyena's face. We spent hours and hours
looking for a way, but she always rejected my sugges-
tions. At last she said, 'I think I've found the answer.
Have you got a maid?'

'Yes,' I said, puzzled.

'There you are then. Ring for your maid, and when
she comes in we'll pounce upon her and tear off her
face. I'll wear her face tonight instead of mine.'

'It's not practical,' I said. 'She'll probably die if she hasn't got a face. Somebody will certainly find the corpse, and we'll be put in prison.'

'I'm hungry enough to eat her,' the hyena replied.

'And the bones?'

'As well,' she said. 'So, it's on?'

'Only if you promise to kill her before tearing off her face. It'll hurt her too much otherwise.'

'All right. It's all the same to me.'

Not without a certain amount of nervousness I rang for Mary, my maid. I certainly wouldn't have done it if I didn't hate having to go to a ball so much. When Mary came in I turned to the wall so as not to see. I must admit it didn't take long. A brief cry, and it was over. While the hyena was eating, I looked out the window. A few minutes later she said, 'I can't eat any more. Her two feet are left over still, but if you have a little bag, I'll eat them later in the day.'

'You'll find a bag embroidered with fleurs-de-lis in the cupboard. Empty out the handkerchiefs you'll find inside, and take it.'

She did as I suggested. Then she said, 'Turn round now and look how beautiful I am.'

In front of the mirror, the hyena was admiring

herself in Mary's face. She had nibbled very neatly all around the face so that what was left was exactly what was needed.

'You've certainly done that very well,' I said.

Towards evening, when the hyena was all dressed up, she declared, 'I really feel in tip-top form. I have a feeling that I shall be a great success this evening.'

When we had heard the music from downstairs for quite some time, I said to her, 'Go on down now, and remember, don't stand next to my mother. She's bound to realise that it isn't me. Apart from her I don't know anybody. Best of luck.' I kissed her as I left her, but she did smell very strong.

Night fell. Tired by the day's emotions, I took a book and sat down by the open window, giving myself up to peace and quiet. I remember that I was reading *Gulliver's Travels* by Jonathan Swift. About an hour later, I noticed the first signs of trouble. A bat flew in at the window, uttering little cries. I am terribly afraid of bats. I hid behind a chair, my teeth chattering. I had hardly gone down on my knees when the sound of beating wings was overcome by a great noise at my door. My mother entered, pale with rage.

'We'd just sat down at table,' she said, 'when that thing sitting in your place got up and shouted, "So I smell a bit strong, what? Well, I don't eat cakes!" Whereupon it tore off its face and ate it. And with one great bound, disappeared through the window.'

The Oval Lady

A very tall thin lady was standing at the window. The window was very high and very thin too. The lady's face was pale and sad. She didn't move, and nothing moved in the window except the pheasant feather in her hair. My eyes kept being drawn to the quivering feather: it was so restless in the window, where nothing was moving!

This was the seventh time I had passed in front of this window. The sad lady hadn't stirred; in spite of the cold that evening, I stopped. Perhaps the furniture in the room was as long and thin as the lady and the window. Perhaps the cat, if there were a cat, would also conform to their elegant proportions. I wanted to know, I was devoured by curiosity, an irresistible desire took hold of me to enter the house, simply to find out.

Before I knew exactly what I was doing, I had

reached the entrance hall. The door closed quietly behind me, and for the first time in my life I found myself inside a stately home. It was overwhelming. For a start, there was such a distinguished silence that I hardly dared to breathe. Then there was the incredible elegance of the furniture and the trinkets. Every chair was at least twice as tall as an ordinary chair, and very much narrower. For these aristocrats, even plates were oval, not round like ordinary people's. The drawing-room, where the sad lady was standing, was adorned with a fireplace, and there was a table laid with teacups and cakes. Near the fire, a teapot waited quietly to be poured.

Seen from the back, the lady seemed even taller. She was at least ten feet tall. The problem was how to speak to her. Begin with the weather, and how bad it was? Too banal. Talk of poetry! But what poetry?

'Madam, do you like poetry?'

'No, I hate poetry,' she answered in a voice stifled with boredom, without turning to me.

'Have a cup of tea, it will make you feel better.'

'I don't drink, I don't eat. It's a protest against my father, the bastard.'

After a quarter of an hour's silence she turned

around, and I was astonished by her youth. She was perhaps sixteen years old.

'You're very tall for your age, Miss. When I was sixteen I wasn't half as tall as you.'

'I don't care. Anyway, give me some tea, but don't tell anyone. Perhaps I'll also have one of those cakes, but whatever you do, remember not to say anything.'

She ate with an absolutely amazing appetite. When she got to the twentieth cake she said, 'Even if I die of hunger, he'll never win. I can see the funeral procession now, with four big black horses, gleaming. They're walking slowly, my little coffin, white in a drift of red roses. And people weeping, weeping.'

She began to weep.

'Look at the little corpse of beautiful Lucretia. And you know, once you're dead, there's nothing very much one can do. I'd like to starve myself to death just to annoy him. What a pig.'

With these words she slowly left the room. I followed her.

When we reached the third floor, we went into an enormous nursery where hundreds of dilapidated and broken toys lay all over the place. Lucretia went up to a wooden horse. In spite of its great age – certainly not much less than a hundred years – it was frozen in a gallop.

'Tartar is my favourite,' she said, stroking the horse's muzzle. 'He loathes my father.'

Tartar rocked himself gracefully on his rockers, and I wondered to myself how he could move by himself. Lucretia looked at him thoughtfully, clasping her hands together.

'He'll travel a very long way like that,' she said. 'And when he comes back he'll tell me something interesting.'

Looking out of doors, I noticed that it was snowing. It was very cold, but Lucretia didn't notice it. A slight sound at the window attracted her attention.

'It's Matilda,' she said. 'I ought to have left the window open. Anyway, it's stifling in here.' With that she broke the windowpanes, and in came the snow with a magpie, which flew around the room three times.

'Matilda talks like this. It's ten years since I split her tongue in two. What a beautiful creature.'

'Beautiful crrrreaturc,' screeched Matilda in a witch's voice. 'Beeeautiful crrrreature.'

Matilda went and perched on Tartar's head. The

horse was still galloping gently. He was covered in snow.

'Did you come to play with us?' enquired Lucretia. 'I'm glad, because I get very bored here. Let's make believe that we're all horses. I'll turn myself into a horse; with some snow, it'll be more convincing. You be a horse too, Matilda.'

'Horse, horse, horse,' yelled Matilda, dancing hysterically on Tartar's head. Lucretia threw herself into the snow, which was already deep, and rolled in it, shouting, 'We are all horses!'

When she emerged, the effect was extraordinary. If I hadn't known that it was Lucretia, I would have sworn that it was a horse. She was beautiful, a blinding white all over, with four legs as fine as needles, and a mane which fell around her long face like water. She laughed with joy and danced madly around in the snow.

'Gallop, gallop, Tartar, but I shall go faster than you.'

Tartar didn't change speed, but his eyes sparkled. One could only see his eyes, for he was covered in snow. Matilda cawed and struck her head against the walls. As for me, I danced a sort of polka so as not to die of cold.

Suddenly I noticed that the door was open, and that an old woman stood framed in the doorway. She had been there perhaps for a long time without my noticing her. She looked at Lucretia with a nasty stare.

'*Stop at once,*' she cried, suddenly trembling with fury. 'What's all this? Eh, my young ladies? Lucretia, you know this game has been strictly forbidden by your father. This ridiculous game. You aren't a child anymore.'

Lucretia danced on, flinging out her four legs dangerously near the old woman; her laughter was piercing.

'*Stop, Lucretia!*'

Lucretia's voice became shriller and shriller. She was doubled up with laughter.

'All right,' said the old woman. 'So you won't obey me, young lady? All right, you'll regret it. I'm going to take you to your father.'

One of her hands was hidden behind her back, but with astonishing speed for someone so old, she jumped on Lucretia's back and forced a bit between her teeth. Lucretia leapt into the air, neighing with rage, but the old woman held on. After that she caught each of us, me by my hair and Matilda by her head, and all four of us were hurled into a frenzied dance. In the corridor, Lucretia kicked out everywhere and smashed pictures and chairs and china. The old woman clung to her back like a limpet to a rock. I was covered in cuts and bruises, and thought Matilda must be dead, for she was fluttering sadly in the old woman's hand like a rag.

We arrived in the dining-room in a veritable orgy of noise. Sitting at the end of a long table, an old gentleman, looking more like a geometric figure than anything else, was finishing his meal. All at once complete silence fell in the room. Lucretia looked at her father with swollen eyes.

'So you're starting up your old tricks again,' he said, cracking a hazelnut. 'Mademoiselle de la Rochefroide did well to bring you here. It's exactly three years and three days since I forbade you to play at horses. This is the seventh time that I have had to punish you, and you are no doubt aware that in our family, seven is the last number. I'm afraid, my dear Lucretia, that this time I shall have to punish you pretty severely.'

The girl, who had taken the appearance of a horse, did not move, but her nostrils quivered.

'What I'm going to do is purely for your own good, my dear.' His voice was very gentle. 'You're too old to play with Tartar. Tartar is for children. I am going to burn him myself, until there's nothing left of him.'

Lucretia gave a terrible cry and fell to her knees. 'Not that, Papa, not that.'

The old man smiled with great sweetness and cracked another hazelnut.

'It's the seventh time, my dear.'

The tears ran from Lucretia's great horse's eyes and carved two channels in her cheeks of snow. She turned such a dazzling white that she shone like a star.

'Have pity, Papa, have pity. Don't burn Tartar.'

Her shrill voice grew thinner and thinner, and she was soon kneeling in a pool of water. I was afraid that she was going to melt away.

'Mademoiselle de la Rochefroide, take Miss Lucretia outside,' said her father, and the old woman took the poor creature, who had become all thin and trembling, out of the room.

I don't think he had noticed I was there. I hid behind the door and heard the old man go up to the nursery. A little later I stopped my ears with my fingers, for the most frightful neighing sounded from above, as if an animal were suffering extreme torture.

The Seventh Horse

A strange-looking creature was hopping about in the midst of a bramble bush. She was caught by her long hair, which was so closely entwined in the brambles that she could move neither backwards nor forwards. She was cursing and hopping till the blood flowed down her body.

'I do not like the look of it,' said one of the two ladies who intended to visit the rose garden.

'It might be a young woman . . . and yet . . .'

'This is my garden,' replied the other, who was as thin and dry as a stick. 'And I strongly object to tres-passers. I expect it is my poor silly little husband who has let her in. He is such a child you know.'

'I've been here for years,' shrieked the creature angrily. 'But you are too stupid to have seen me.'

'Impertinent as well,' remarked the first lady, who was called Miss Myrtle. 'I think you had better call the gardener, Mildred. I don't think it is quite safe to go so near. The creature seems to have no modesty.'

Hevalino tugged angrily at her hair as if she would like to get at Mildred and her companion. The two ladies turned to go, not before they had exchanged a long look of hate with Hevalino.

The spring evening was lengthening before the gardener came to set Hevalino free.

'John,' said Hevalino, lying down on the grass, 'can you count up to seven? Do you know that I can hate for seventy-seven million years without stopping for rest. Tell those miserable people that they are doomed.' She trailed off towards the stable where she lived, muttering as she went: 'Seventy-seven, seventy-seven.'

There were certain parts of the garden where all the flowers, trees and plants grew tangled together. Even on the hottest days these places were in blue shadow. There were deserted figures overgrown with moss, still fountains and old toys, decapitated and destitute. Nobody went there except Hevalino; she would kneel and eat the short grass and watch a fascinating fat bird who never moved away from his shadow. He let his shadow glide around him as the day went by and over around him when there was a moon. He always sat with his hairy mouth wide open, and moths and little insects would fly in and out.

Hevalino went to see the bird dining the night after she was caught in the brambles. A retinue of six horses accompanied her. They walked seven times around the fat bird in silence.

'Who's there?' said the bird eventually, in a whistling voice.

'It is I, Hevalino, with my six horses.'

'You are keeping me awake with your stumping and snorting,' came the plaintive reply. 'If I cannot sleep I can see neither the past nor the future. I shall waste away if you won't go away and let me sleep.'

'They are going to come and kill you,' said Hevalino. 'You had better keep awake. I heard somebody say you would be roasted in hot fat, stuffed with parsley and onions, and then eaten.'

The corpulent bird cast an apprehensive eye on Hevalino, who was watching him closely.

'How do you know?' breathed the bird. 'Just tell me that.'

'You are much too fat to fly,' continued Hevalino

relentlessly. 'If you tried to fly you'd be like a fat toad doing his death dance.'

'How do you know this?' screamed the bird. 'They can't know where I am. I've been here for seventy-seven years.'

'They don't know yet . . . not yet.' Hevalino had her face close to his open beak; her lips were drawn back and the bird could see her long wolves' teeth.

His fat little body quivered like a jelly.

'What do you want of me?'

Hevalino gave a sort of crooked smile. 'Ah, that's better.' She and the six horses made a circle around the bird and watched him with their prominent and relentless eyes.

'I want to know exactly what is going on in the house,' said she. 'And be quick about it.' The bird cast a frightened look around him, but the horses had sat down. There was no escape. He became wet with sweat and the feathers clung, draggled, to his fat stomach.

'I cannot say,' he said at last in a strangled voice. 'Something terrible will befall us if I say what I can see.'

'Roasted in hot fat and eaten,' said Hevalino.

'You are mad to want to know things that do not concern you!'

'I am waiting,' said Hevalino. The bird gave a long convulsive shudder and turned his eyes, which had become bulging and sightless, to the east.

'They are at dinner,' he said eventually, and a great black moth flew out of his mouth.

'The table is laid for three people. Mildred and her husband have begun to eat their soup. She is watching him suspiciously. "I found something unpleasant in the garden today," she says, laying down her spoon; I doubt if she will eat any more now.

' "What was that?" asks he. "Why do you look so angry?"

'Miss Myrtle has now come into the room. She looks from one to the other. She seems to guess what they are discussing, for she says: "Yes, really, Philip, I think you ought to be more careful whom you let into the garden."

' "What are you talking about?" he says angrily. "How do you expect me to stop anything if I don't know what I am stopping?"

' "It was an unpleasant-looking creature half

naked and caught in a bramble bush. I had to turn my eyes away."

' "You let this creature free, of course?"

' "Indeed I did not. I consider it just as well that she was trapped as she was. By the cruel look on her face I should judge she would have done us serious harm."

' "What! You left this poor creature trapped in the brambles? Mildred, there are times when you revolt me. I am sick of you pottering around the village and annoying the poor with your religious preamble, and now when you see a poor thing in your own garden you do nothing but shudder with false modesty."

'Mildred gives a shocked cry and covers her face with a slightly soiled handkerchief. "Philip, why do you say such cruel things to me, your wife?"

'Philip, with an expression of resigned annoyance asks, "Try and describe this creature. Is it an animal or a woman?"

' "I can say no more," sobs the wife. "After what you have said to me I feel faint."

' "You should be more careful," whispers Miss Myrtle. "In her delicate condition!"

' "What do you mean 'delicate condition'?" asks

Philip irritably. "I do wish people would say what they mean."

' "Why surely you must know." Miss Myrtle simpers. "You are going to become a daddy in a short time . . ."

'Philip goes white with rage. "I won't stand these fatuous lies. It is quite impossible that Mildred is pregnant. She has not graced my bed for five whole years, and unless the Holy Ghost is in the house I don't see how it came about. For Mildred is unpleasantly virtuous, and I cannot imagine her abandoning herself to anybody."

' "Mildred, is this true?" says Miss Myrtle, trembling with delicious expectation. Mildred shrieks and sobs: "He is a liar. I am going to have a darling little baby in three months."

'Philip flings down his spoon and serviette and gets to his feet. "For the seventh time in seven days I shall finish my dinner upstairs," says he, and stops for an instant as if his words have awakened some memory. He puts it away from him and shakes his head. "All I ask is that you don't come whining after me," he says to his wife and quits the room. She shrieks: "Philip, my darling little husband; come back

35

and eat your soup, I promise I won't be naughty anymore."

' "Too late," comes the voice of Philip from the staircase, "too late now."

'He goes slowly up to the top of the house with his eyes looking a long way ahead of him. His face is strained as if in the effort of listening to faraway voices chattering between nightmares and dead reality. He reaches the attic at the top of the house, where he seats himself on an old trunk. I believe that the trunk is filled with ancient laces, frilly knickers, and dresses. But they are old and torn; there is a black moth making his dinner on them as Philip sits staring at the window. He considers a stuffed hedge-pig on the mantelpiece, who looks worn out with suffering. Philip seems to be smothered with the atmosphere of this attic; he flings open the window and gives a long . . .'

Here the bird paused, and a long sickening neigh rent the night. The six horses leapt to their feet and replied in their piercing voices. Hevalino stood stock-still, with her lips drawn back and her nostrils quivering. 'Philip, the friend of the horses . . .' The six horses thundered off towards the stable, as if obeying an age-old summons. Hevalino, with a shuddering sigh, followed, her hair streaming behind her.

Philip was at the stable door as they arrived. His face was luminous and as white as snow. He counted seven horses as they galloped by. He caught the seventh by the mane and leapt onto her back. The mare galloped as if her heart would burst. And all the time Philip was in a great ecstasy of love; he felt he had grown onto the back of this beautiful black mare, and that they were one creature.

At the crack of dawn all the horses were back in their places. And the little wrinkled groom was rubbing off the caked sweat and mud of the night. His creased face smiled wisely as he rubbed his charges with infinite care. He appeared not to notice the master, who stood alone in an empty stall. But he knew he was there.

'How many horses have I?' said Philip at last.

'Six, sir,' said the little groom, without ceasing to smile.

That night the corpse of Mildred was found near the stable. One would believe that she had been trampled to death . . . and yet 'They are all as gentle as lambs,' said the little groom. If Mildred had been pregnant there was no sign of it as she was stuffed into a respectable black coffin. However nobody could explain the presence of a small misshapen foal that had found its way into the seventh empty stall.

My Flannel Knickers

Thousands of people know my flannel knickers, and though I know this may seem flirtatious, it is not. I am a saint.

The 'Sainthood', I may say, was actually forced upon me. If anyone would like to avoid becoming holy, they should immediately read this entire story.

I live on an island. This island was bestowed upon me by the government when I left prison. It is not a desert island, it is a traffic island in the middle of a busy boulevard, and motors thunder past on all sides day and night.

So . . .

The flannel knickers are well-known. They are hung at midday on a wire from the red, green and yellow automatic lights. I wash them every day, and they have to dry in the sun.

Apart from the flannel knickers, I wear a gentleman's tweed jacket for golfing. It was given to me, and the gym shoes. No socks. Many people recoil from my undistinguished appearance, but if they have been told about me (mainly in the tourists' guide), they make a pilgrimage, which is quite easy.

Now I must trace the peculiar events that brought me to this condition. Once I was a great beauty and attended all sorts of cocktail-drinking, prize-giving-and-taking, artistic demonstrations and other casually hazardous gatherings organized for the purpose of people wasting other people's time. I was always in demand and my beautiful face would hang suspended over fashionable garments, smiling continually. An ardent heart, however, beat under the fashionable costumes and this very ardent heart was like an open tap pouring quantities of hot water over anybody who asked. This wasteful process soon took its toll on my beautiful smiling face. My teeth fell out. The original structure of the face became blurred and then began to fall away from the bones in small, ever-increasing folds. I sat and watched the process with a mixture of slighted vanity and acute depression. I was, I thought, solidly installed in my lunar plexus, within clouds of sensitive vapour.

If I happened to smile at my face in the mirror, I could objectively observe the fact that I had only three teeth left and these were beginning to decay.

Consequently I went to the dentist. Not only did he cure the three remaining teeth but he also presented me with a set of false teeth, cunningly mounted on a pink plastic chassis. When I had paid a sufficiently large quantity of my diminishing wealth, the teeth were mine and I took them home and put them into my mouth.

The face seemed to regain some of its absolutely-irresistible-attraction, although the folds were of course still there. From the lunar plexus I arose like a hungry trout and was caught fast on the sharp barbed hook that hangs inside all once-very-beautiful faces.

A thin magnetic mist formed between myself, the face, and clear perception. This is what I saw in the mist. 'Well, well. I really was beginning to petrify in that old lunar plexus. This must be me, this beautiful, smiling, fully toothed creature. There I was, sitting in the dark bloodstream like a mummified foetus with no love at all. Here I am, back in the rich world, where I can palpitate again, jump up and down in the nice warm swimming pool of outflowing emotion, the more bathers the merrier. I Shall Be Enriched.'

All these disastrous thoughts were multiplied and reflected in the magnetic mist. I stepped in, wearing my face, now back in the old enigmatic smile which had always turned sour in the past.

No sooner trapped than done.

Smiling horribly, I returned to the jungle of faces each ravenously trying to eat each other.

Here I might explain the process that actually takes place in this sort of jungle. Each face is provided with greater or smaller mouths, armed with different kinds of sometimes natural teeth. (Anybody over forty and toothless should be sensible enough to be quietly knitting an original new body, instead of wasting the cosmic wool.) These teeth bar the way to a gaping throat, which disgorges whatever it swallows back into the foetid atmosphere.

The bodies over which these faces are suspended serve as ballast to the faces. As a rule they are carefully covered with colours and shapes in current 'fashion'. This 'fashion' is a devouring idea launched by another face snapping with insatiable hunger for money and notoriety. The bodies, in constant misery and supplication, are generally ignored and only used for ambulation of the face. As I said, for ballast.

Once, however, that I bared my new teeth, I realized that something had gone wrong. For after a very short period of enigmatic smiling, the smile became quite stiff and fixed, while the face slipped away from its bonish mooring, leaving me clutching desperately to a soft grey mask over a barely animated body.

The strange part of the affair now reveals itself. The jungle faces, instead of recoiling in horror from what I already knew to be a sad sight, approached me and started to beg me for something which I thought I had not got.

Puzzled, I consulted my friend, a Greek.

He said: 'They think you have woven a complete face and body and are in constant possession of excess amounts of cosmic wool. Even if this is not so, the very fact that you know about the wool makes them determined to steal it.'

'I have wasted practically the entire fleece,' I told him. 'And if anybody steals from me now I shall die and disintegrate totally.'

'Three-dimensional life,' said the Greek, 'is formed by attitude. Since by their attitude they expect you to have quantities of wool, you are three-dimensionally forced to "Sainthood", which means you must spin your body and teach the faces how to spin theirs.'

The compassionate words of the Greek filled me with fear. I am a face myself. The quickest way of retiring from social face-eating competition occurred to me when I attacked a policeman with my strong steel umbrella. I was quickly put into prison, where I spent months in health-giving meditation and compulsive exercise.

My exemplary conduct in prison moved the head wardress to an excess of bounty, and that is how the government presented me with the island, after a small and distinguished ceremony in a remote corner of the Protestant cemetery.

So here I am on the island with all sizes of mechanical artefacts whizzing by in every conceivable direction, even overhead.

Here I sit.

The Skeleton's Holiday

The skeleton was as happy as a madman whose straitjacket had been taken off. He felt liberated at being able to walk without flesh. The mosquitoes didn't bite him anymore. He didn't have to have his hair cut. He was neither hungry nor thirsty, hot nor cold. He was far from the lizard of love. For some time, a German, a professor of chemistry, had been eyeing him, thinking he might convert him into delicious ersatz: dynamite, strawberry jam, garnished sauerkraut. The skeleton knew how to give him the slip, by letting fall a young zeppelin bone, on which the professor pounced, reciting chemical hymns and covering the bone with hot kisses.

The skeleton's lodgings had an ancient head and modern feet. The ceiling was the sky, the floor the earth. It was painted white and decorated with snowballs in which a heart beat. He looked like a transparent monument dreaming of an electric breast, and gazed without eyes, with a pleasant and invisible smile, into the inexhaustible supply of silence that surrounds our star.

The skeleton didn't like disasters, but to suggest that life did have its hazardous moments, he had placed an enormous thimble in the middle of his fine apartment, on which he sat from time to time like a real philosopher. Sometimes he danced a few steps to the tune of Saint-Saëns's 'Danse Macabre'. But he did it with such grace, with such guilelessness, in the manner of midnight dances in romantic, old-fashioned graveyards, that nobody seeing him would have thought of anything unpleasant.

Satisfied, he contemplated the Milky Way, the army of bones that encircles our planet. It sparkles, glitters, shines with all its myriad little skeletons that dance, jump, turn somersaults, do their duty. They welcome the dead from the thousand fields of honour, the honour of hyenas, adders, crocodiles, bats, lice, toads, spiders, tapeworms, scorpions. They provide first counsel, guide the first steps of the newly dead, who are wretched in their abandonment, like the new-born. Our repugnant eminent cohorts, co-brothers, co-sisters, co-uncles and aunts who smell of wild boar and have noses encrusted with dry oysters, are transformed upon dying, into skeletons. Have you heard the appalling moan of the dead in slaughter? It's the terrible disillusionment of the newly born dead, who'd hoped for and deserved eternal sleep but find themselves tricked, caught up in an endless machinery of pain and sorrow.

The skeleton got up every morning, clean as a Gillette blade. He decorated his bones with herbs, brushed his teeth with ancestor marrow, and lacquered his nails with Fatma Red. In the evening, at cocktail time, he went to the café on the corner, where he read the *Necromancer's Journal*, the paper favoured by high-toned corpses. Often he amused himself by playing dirty tricks. Once he pretended to be thirsty and asked for writing materials; he emptied the inkpot between his jaws into his carcass: the ink stained and spotted his white bones. Another time he went into a joke shop and bought himself a supply of those Parisian pleasantries, imitation turds. One evening he put some in his chamber pot, and his servant never got over the shock in the morning: to think that a skeleton who neither ate nor drank did his business like the rest of us.

It happened that one day the skeleton drew some hazelnuts that walked about on little legs across mountains, that spit frogs out of mouth, eye, ear, nose, and other openings and holes. The skeleton took fright like a skeleton meeting a skeleton in bright daylight. Quickly he had a pumpkin detector grow on his head, with a day side like patchouli bread and a night side like the egg of Columbus, and set off, half reassured, to see a fortune-teller.